SUPERTATO

NIGHT OF THE LIVING VEG

Meet Sue and Paul:

Sue Hendra and Paul Linnet have been making books together
since 2009 when they came up with *Barry the Fish with Fingers*,
and since then they haven't stopped. If you've ever wondered
which one does the writing and which does the illustrating,
wonder no more . . . they both do both!

To our lovely friend Steve

SIMON & SCHUSTER

First published in Great Britain in 2021 by Simon & Schuster UK Ltd • 1st Floor, 222 Gray's Inn Road, London, WC1X 8HB

978-1-4711-8923-4 (PB) • 978-1-4711-8925-8 (eBook) • 978-1-3985-0889-7 (eAudio) • Printed in China • 10 9 8 7 6 5 4 3 2

SUPERTATO

NIGHT OF THE LIVING VEG

SUE HENDRA
PAUL LINNET

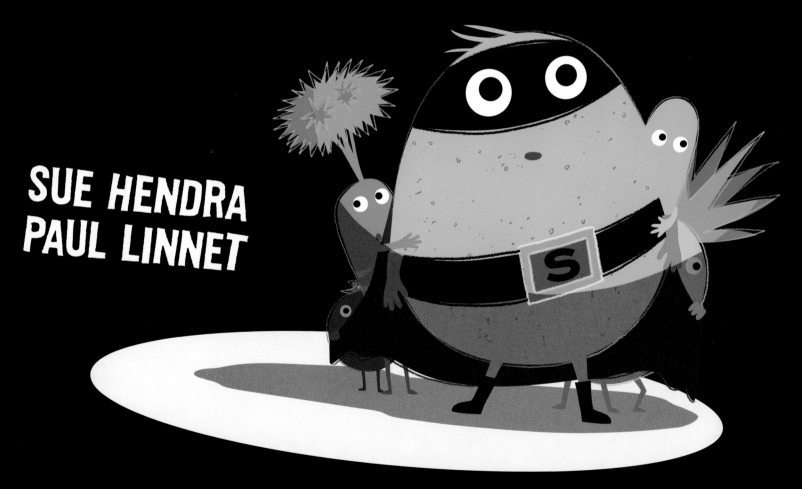

SIMON & SCHUSTER
London   New York   Sydney   Toronto   New Delhi

It was fright-time in the supermarket and Tomato was trembling,

Cucumber was quivering

Well, not immediately, but it did eventually . . .

SLEEPY - TATO
TO THE RESCUE!

"What's going on, veggies?
Why are you all
so frightened?"

"B . . . b . . . b . . . because there's a creepy robot!" gasped Carrot.

"And a spooky witch!"
cried Tomato.

"And a ghastly ghostie!"
wailed Cucumber.

"No, no, no. That's not a creepy robot, Carrot. It's just some boxes of cereal and biscuits.

And that's not a spooky witch, Tomato. It's just an old mop and a traffic cone.

And that's not a ghastly ghostie, Cucumber. It's just . . .

. . . Pineapple! Whatever are you doing up there with the towels and the flannels?"

"We're hiding from the scary things, Supertato!"

"At the moment, Pineapple, you and Orange ARE the scary things! Now, down you come.

Look, veggies, there really is nothing to be frightened of. I think it's time we all got back to our beds."

"But what about the scary noises, Supertato?"

"What scary noi . . ."

Hmmm . . .
thought Supertato.
Perhaps the veggies
had a point.

"Now, let's not get carried away.
There's clearly something
behind those boxes ... Wooooooooooooo

SOMEONE is trying to scare us,
and I bet I know who!"

"Well, it's not me if that's what you're thinking," said The Evil Pea, huddling nervously with the veggies.

"Oh."

"Well if it's not the Pea," shrieked Tomato, "then WHAT is it?"

Everyone started to panic.

"Now, hang on, everybody," said Supertato. But before he could continue . . . .

"WAIT!" shouted Broccoli. "I know what it is . . ."

Everyone stopped and listened closely.

"Legend tells of the Living Veg –
late at night, when no one is around . . .

they roam the deserted aisles
of the supermarket . . .

looking for sleepy little veggies,
and when they find them,

they . . ."

"That's quite enough of that, thank you, Broccoli," said Supertato, firmly. "This is getting completely out of hand. Let's all calm down and . . ."

"Shhhhhh!" Broccoli shushed him. "Everyone, listen!"

And that was when they heard it . . . the shuffling . . .

"It's the Living Veg – they're EVERYWHERE!"

"Something's got me!" said a voice.

"Something's got who?" yelled Tomato.

"Me!" shouted Supertato. "They've got me by the cape!
Can anyone reach the light switch?"

Cucumber made a leap for it,
and all of a sudden . . .

. . . they saw them!

But it wasn't the Living Veg –
it was hundreds of tiny peas,
groaning and moaning like Zom-peas.

"Supertato, please help us.
We can't sleep!" wailed
the peas, still pulling
on Supertato's cape.

"We never get read a bedtime story."

"Evil Pea, you should know better," said Supertato. "No wonder your peas are shuffling about, moaning. How do you expect them to go to sleep without a bedtime story?

Surely everybody knows how important it is to read to little ones at bedtime?

Now, come on, everyone. Follow me!

It's story time!
Now, is everyone snuggly?"

"Yes, Supertato!"

"OK, then I'll begin.
It was night-time in the supermarket . . ."

If you like

SUPERTATO

NIGHT OF THE LIVING VEG

you'll love these other

adventures from

SUE HENDRA & PAUL LINNET

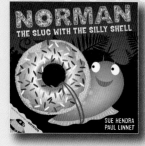